STE/

FLASHES

AN ANTHOLOGY

A collection of Steampunk and Nepali infused flash fiction short stories, with related articles, photographs and artwork, raising funds for and awareness of New Futures Nepal.

1

Paperback ISBN: 978-0-9565147-1-4

Cover artwork © Tenebrous Texts, from a photograph by Steven C. Davis.

Published by Tenebrous Texts

www.tenebroustexts.com
mail@tenebroustexts.com

Index of contents

Introduction

On 25th April 2015, just before midday, Nepalese standard time, a major earthquake struck Nepal. On 12th May 2015, a second major earthquake struck Nepal. The death toll from both is in the thousands, with many more injured or lost. Homes were destroyed, villages wiped out, and many trails, a source of tourist income, were erased, with risks of landslides remaining.

New Futures Nepal are not an emergency-response charity. They work with orphaned and disabled youngsters and adults in Nepal and Northern India, and have an outreach project and have funded or helped fund a number of projects supporting and helping the Nepalese long before these events.

But when the earthquakes struck, they were there on the ground. The work they have done supporting disabled or disadvantaged children has given the children hope, life, and a future. And that is what the charity is about.

And, having visited Nepal ourselves and supporting New Futures Nepal, we couldn't stand by and do nothing. And so, we give you – Steam *Flashes*.

Steam *Flashes* is a collection of flash fiction short stories. Flash fiction offers a challenge in terms of the word count – 500 words in this instance, although we did allow some which exceeded that.

The anthology was officially announced at Southcart Books, Walsall, on Saturday 18th July. In addition to the authors reading from their works (some of which are reproduced here with their kind permission), there was also tea duelling and talks from Kevin Cooper and Miranda T. about making and creating things, plus photographs from Creating Magic, in addition to a raffle for New Futures Nepal, and you will find more about all of this throughout this book.

Photo © Craig Beas

And what an anthology it has turned out to be! From the intrigue of Thea Bradbury's 'The Resurrectionist' to a take on the Kumari Devi, the living Goddess, by Danielle Miller, from Theresa Derwin's emotive 'Why Did the Elephant Cross the Road', to mechanical Yak and stories of Yetis sought and not found, to tales of Steamships and airships, from Stu Tovell's very clever tale, to a simple imagining of the moment when the earthquake struck from Steven C. Davis, from C. Harper-Leigh's reworking of 'The Rime of the Ancient Mariner' to Adam Millard's tale of the future of books and James Josiah's 'Where The Poppies Bloom' about Death and an immortal Being – to the lovely and amazing photographs and artwork from Chelle Tovell and S. J. Stewart, and to the 'how to' articles from Kev Cooper and Miranda T., showing you how to create something original for yourself, there is something for everyone. Not forgetting, of course, the photos, courtesy of Craig Beas, LM Cooke and Steven C. Davis.

And that just leaves it up to me to say thank you to everyone involved, both at the launch event at Southcart Books (the only independent bookshop in Walsall) and afterwards, online and in real life. Particular thanks to all those who have generously donated their works to this anthology, we hope you like the results, and thank you for sharing your creativity!

Xavier Trulock
CEO, Tenebrous Texts

New Futures Nepal

New Futures Nepal is a small but effective charity run entirely by volunteers *(as described by our patrons Sir Chris Bonnington and Doug Scott)*. Our aims are to empower disadvantaged children and adults of Nepal by raising funds for initiatives that promote health, education and independence. We work to help and support social integration for children with disabilities to live in the community and within safe and loving homes. We adopt a 'hands on, personal approach', keep our administration costs low and work with local charities and organisations worldwide to facilitate the charity's goals.

We have three major long term projects, they are The Hope Centre in Kathmandu, a childrens home where we care for about 40 children, Hornbeam House in Kalimpong, West Bengal, a home for 12 children and young adults and the Bhaktaphur Parents Run Day Care Centre in Kathmandu who support families of children with Cerebral Palsy. These three projects provide employment for over 15 people. We fund schooling and further education costs for the children in both homes in Kathmandu and Kalimpong. We also provide funds under a 'Lifelines' scheme for one off projects or emergencies such as this year's catastrophic earthquakes in Nepal.

The charity was registered in 2003 and in its first year raised over £3000 which saved the sight of one little girl, restored mobility to another and allowed us to launch a project to build our own children's home on the outskirts of Kathmandu. We raised over £100,000 to complete this project and The Hope Centre family moved into their new home in 2005. Several of the original children are now working and living independent lives thereby realising the charity's aims and fulfilling the children's dreams.

In the past 12 years we have funded numerous surgical interventions for disabled children, distributed educational material, DVDs and books to thousands of children in remote areas, funded a clean water project in rural India and provided emergency earthquake relief for hundreds of families. In 2014 we opened our second bespoke children's home in Kalimpong, West Bengal.
Since 2003 we have gone on to raise over £1,250,000, all of which has gone towards our projects in Nepal and India. Our overheads are

covered by the government tax refund Gift Aid scheme.

The charity's original trustees still form part of today's management body and remain as passionate and committed as they were on day one. They are supported by over 50 loyal and energetic supporters who raise funds in inventive and exciting ways. We could not continue to work as effectively as we do without the help of these tireless volunteers. If you are interested in helping please get in touch at info@newfuturesnepal.org.

Thanks
Lynne McCutcheon, Chair, New Futures Nepal
www.newfuturesnepal.org

Photo (c) Steven C. Davis

Why Did the Elephant Cross the Road?
By Theresa Derwin

My Nepalese man-servant Badri assisted my ascension onto the monstrously huge beast that stood before me. We were not about to use a steam-carriage I was informed, as the topography was not suitable, and the mammal before me was deemed to be more reliable.

Its huge grey trunk swung upwards towards where I sat side saddle, then shocked me as it twirled and curled itself around my hand, almost with affection. I dropped my reticule in surprise and laughed. What a magnificent beast. This elephant was a truly regal creature. His name was Mahadeva. Badri told me the creature was named for Lord Shiva.

I knew little of Nepalese customs, I was here after all on an academic exploration, yet I had heard of the name Shiva.

"Yes, Madame," Badri told me as he reached up, returning my reticule, "Mahadeva was the transformer. The 'Auspicious One.' You are fortunate to be favoured by the old one."

I laughed. "Yes indeed, he does seem to like me," I said, patting the elephant's rough hide.

Mahadeva responded with a bellow, again reaching up and twisting around my hand.

I had only been in Nepal a day, yet there was something about this strange land and the creature I was about to ride upon that appealed to me.

We began our trek through this fertile, verdant land from Kathmandu. Green, lush hills that resembled curvaceous staircases, the mountainous terrain in the background with their snow-capped peaks, magnificent temples; ornate gospels made of terracotta erected to honour the Hindu gods and Budda. It was a myriad of colour and life, and I felt my breath catch as Badri led us through the city towards the hills, whilst I held on tight to my friendly mammoth.

At night we set up base camp amidst the hills, in old tents that smelt most foul. By the second day of the trek I had abandoned my bustle and skirts in favour of a gentleman's casual attire; long trousers, shirt and a waistcoat. I did indeed feel underdressed, yet, I must admit, much more comfortable for the journey ahead.

It was on the third day of my exploration, and my endeavour to help the orphans of the region, that my dear and newest friend Mahadeva stopped at a stream and refused to move.

The stream was barely a trickle, but before it, was a temple for one of the many gods of Nepal. Badri attempted to move the beast forward but he would not budge. I had built a rapport with my behemoth of a companion, so thought me to encourage him to move.

"Now Mahadeva, what is this nonsense? You must move my friend. We must reach the orphanage before dark."

Mahadeva snorted at me, sucking up water from the stream then showering me so I was soggy.

"Oh! Mahdi," I protested, "that was uncalled for. Please, why won't you move forward?"

"Because," Mahadeva said in a load trumpet-like voice, "I too have duties." Then, into the distance behind the temple, "Son, are you there?"

I gasped, grabbing the ears of my faithful friend, in shock.

"Wha –" I stumbled, "what? Badri, do you jest?!"

"Not I, Madame', said Badri. "I am here to serve my Lord."

Had I been hearing things? Had the humidity of our travels affected me? Was I about to have an attack of the vapours?

"Fear not, Mrs Cooke, I will not harm you," said my elephant again wrapping his trunk around my arm. "You do not imagine what you hear or see. I come to give you a gift for the children you seek to rescue."

My head momentarily swum, but it was not long before I adjusted. Mahdi had treated me well these last few days, why would it change now?

"That is well then," I said, removing my hands from his ears and patting his head.

It was at this moment that the new god strode towards us; its rotund body, graced also with an elephant's head, approached us. Mahdi removed his trunk from my arm twisting it around the new creature's trunk. They entwined their trunks for a few minutes seeming to share an interior monologue with each other.

Then Mahdi spoke to me again.

"Dear Lady, meet my son, Ganesh. He is the remover of obstacles, and patron of letters and learning. We have talked, and he has agreed to help you in your schooling of the children. You will find a gentleman at the orphanage when you arrive. You will not recognise him, but he will be my son in human form.

He is there to help you build bridges, dear Lady.

These children, these orphans, who have endured much hardship will enjoy life again.

They will have plentiful food, instruments with which to learn.

They will grow, they will work, they will marry, they will have children of their own.

And those children will also learn, become more than society has deemed they should be.

Will you help my son, Mrs Cooke?

Will you help him to build new futures?"

Mahdi finished speaking, and I could hear his smile.

A strange warmth settled over me.

This was my future, my destiny.

To build new futures for the children of Nepal.

Theresa Derwin was born and bred in Birmingham, raised by her Dad on a diet of Hammer double bills, Tango and popcorn. She writes horror, fantasy and SF. She has had over twenty anthology places and two collections printed. Her forthcoming collection Wolf at the Door is due out from KnightWatch Press 2016, as well as a novella God's Vengeance from Crystal Lake Publishing.

The Explorer
By Kev Cooper

A strange device was presented to me recently by an old friend, he being aware of my predilection for such items. Sad to say he had not much concerned my conscience of late, aware as I was that he had been gone from our shores these many years.

I'd last seen him at my club, 'The Thaumaturgists', some considerable number of years ago. He'd been brimming with scarcely contained excitement concerning an expedition upon which he was about to embark. I had wished him good luck and Godspeed, though I was unable to elicit much information as he proved very circumspect regarding his destination.

Little had been heard of his whereabouts in the ensuing years and although I was on occasion a little perturbed by the length of his absence, I ascribed this to the unknown reaches to which I assumed he had departed. For in spite of the many wonders of modern science and the ingenious methods of communicating over long distances, such as the heliograph and the Aetheric tintinabulator, they have their limits when it comes to communicating across continents.

Imagine then my astonishment when 'the explorer' as I shall henceforth refer to him, showed up at my residence just a few days ago.

Apart from looking older due to the passage of the intervening years, he was not much changed, though I fancy there was a world weary air about him as of one who had seen many amazing sights on his travels.

After greeting me effusively, we retired to the library where over a glass of whisky he proceeded to tell me something of his adventures. This is neither the time nor the place to reveal all that he imparted that night, but about two years ago, and some eight years into his adventure 'the explorer' had been offered accommodation aboard the airship Pythagorea. It was bound for Heliolopolis which would then leave my friend within striking distance of his next port of call.

Unfortunate circumstances overtook them while they were still some 1000 miles from their destination. Due to a mechanical failure the airship was forced to tether briefly for repairs at an unknown island, or what appeared to be left of an island which had suffered some catastrophic accident, possibly volcanic in nature.

Whilst the crew set about the repairs, some of the passengers, 'the explorer' among them, proceeded to do a little investigating of the location. Among the rubble strewn about, they discerned what appeared to be the ruins of some sort of dock. This they declared would have been impossible as it would have meant prior to the explosion or volcanic eruption the dock would not only have been subterranean, but also underwater, clearly a ludicrous idea as the area had once been part of an extensive mountain range. There was other evidence of the long gone inhabitants and it was here that my friend found the remains of what can only be described as scientific instruments. The most complete of these devices is that which he gave to me. I have undertaken some modest repairs and a small amount of restoration work though not enough to in any way alter the basic structure or operation of the apparatus.

We may never be certain of its specific function or purpose but the device is obviously intended for studying the effects of light upon various coloured elements. I can ascribe no particular relevance to the images it produces though they are of a fascinating and pleasing arrangement.

The identity of the original owner and perhaps creator remains unknown; the writing etched into the corroded brass name plate is not clearly decipherable though evidently he was a sea captain, the name might be interpreted as 'Nero' or 'Nemo' and the date and location recorded as Nepal 1873.

I was born with the urge to create; it seems to be hereditary. I was also born a Steampunk – though it didn't have a descriptor for most of my life – it may be due to the fact that I was young while the age of steam was still extant. I vividly remember being enveloped in clouds of smoke and steam as the train passed underneath bridges. Art College introduced me to modern art movements but I still can't resist the pull of Victoriana, Gothic architecture and Art Nouveau. I'm also compelled to turn my hand to most forms of creativity.

View from Annapurna Base
Camp (4,130 m). 2002

Along the descent from the
Annapurna Base Camp 2002

Children of the Hope
Centre, 2002.

The Resurrectionist
By Thea Bradbury

Darkness and wind over the mountains. Ice crystals battering the ship's envelope at eight thousand feet. Sergeant Louisa Okoye hates to fly, but she is a servant of the law and right now, the law requires her to procure the services of a resurrectionist.

Onlookers throng the airfield as the ship touches down; craning their necks to see inside the gondola. Louisa would have preferred to do this more subtly, but there is only so much subtlety you can command when you are six foot four, uniformed, and towing a coffin.

There are currently eight resurrectionists in the employ of His Majesty's Government of Great Britain and the Colonies. The precise value of 'employ' varies significantly from case to case, and few of them obey the laws on keeping the government informed of their location. Hence a significant headache for the Metropolitan Police when Home Secretary Geoffrey Herschfield was found dead in his bedchamber without a mark on him last night. Hence, Kathmandu.

The resurrectionist is so thin she can see his ribs through his shirt. He speaks English with an accent that is neither British nor Nepali nor anything else.

"I will require something from you as a guarantee of the ritual's efficacy." The words are smooth, practiced. As familiar to him as they are to her.

"Of course. What?"

The resurrectionist glances dispassionately at the stiff white face of the man in the coffin, the grey stubble piercing the shrinking skin of his chin. Louisa waits, hopes he will only ask for blood. She can't muster sweat at this altitude, and spit and hair are too weak to wake a corpse. She does not allow herself to think about the other thing he might demand, his fingers curling inside her. She reminds herself that she is here to bring justice to the perpetrator, no matter what it takes.

"Hair," he says at last. She starts, does not quite contradict him. To raise Herschfield by hair alone requires more power than can plausibly exist in the frail body of the resurrectionist. He smiles. "You doubt me?"

She does not respond. Takes the scissors he proffers, chops off a generous chunk of her braid. He smiles again.

A little-known fact: a resurrectionist does not literally raise the dead. Rather, he – and in Louisa's experience it is invariably a he – channels their consciousness for a brief moment, long enough to vouchsafe a single piece of information to whoever is listening. A piece of information such as the name of their murderer.

At least, that is what happens if the procedure succeeds. Louisa has seen it fail, too, and it is not an experience she wishes to repeat.

Thick, scented smoke billows out of the fireplace, filling the workshop. Louisa breathes as shallowly as possible, prepares herself for the screams of a soul in torment as the resurrectionist does his work. He is nothing more than a dim outline poised above the coffin. Any minute now, he will fall to the floor and writhe as every resurrectionist before him has done, clawing at his skin as though coated in grave dirt.

And then, without her so much as having blinked, he is standing directly in front of her. He opens his eyes, and they are dead black from pupil to sclera.
"Henry Worsley," he says in a voice which is not his own. Then he collapses, directly into Louisa's arms.

Henry Worsley is the Lord Chief Justice of Greater London. Henry Worsley is at the top of the chain of authority that begins with Louisa and the Metropolitan Police. Henry Worsley killed Geoffrey Herschfield. A corpse cannot lie, and thus neither can a resurrectionist.

Louisa recalls the impressive fall in crime over the three years since Worsley took up his position. Recalls whispers behind closed doors at the station and shadows in the London fog. Thinks about the man lying in the coffin, the power he commanded, putty-pale skin and not a mark on him when he died. Her own blood surging sure and fragile through her veins. She makes a decision.

The resurrectionist opens his eyes, and they are human again.

"You got your name," he says. It is not a question.

"Magnus Wiseacre," she replies. A small-time gangster on the edge of the big-time, the force has been keeping him in reserve for years, waiting until they needed someone to pin something on. No-one will doubt her. And if they do – well, Sir Worsley will be the final arbiter of that.

The resurrectionist stares at her for a very long time. She thinks of mountain cold and mountain solitude and the prayer flags twisting in the wind outside. Thinks of tearing the chevrons off her shoulder and starting over. Finally, the resurrectionist smiles and stands up.

"Magnus Wiseacre," he says. "Well, well."

The stars are shining above her when she leaves the workshop, coffin in tow. She does not look back.

Thea Bradbury is an Oxford student whose increasingly creative attempts to avoid doing actual work have resulted in, among other misadventures, a story for the Steam Flashes anthology. In the course of pursuing a degree in German literature, they have managed to get sidetracked by everything from urban planning to arts journalism, to the ongoing bewilderment and frustration of their professors. They recently started writing a dissertation about performance art and are still trying to figure out how to stop.

Creating Magic
Images © Chelle Tovell

As a young girl I remember sitting on my Nana's knee and looking at old photos in the Family album. I guess that is where my love of photographs (especially Black and White) first began.

I have always enjoyed taking photographs and enhancing them by editing, but only started taking it more seriously in April 2014.

I hope you enjoy my work.

Chelle Tovell

To see more of Chelle's wonderful work, go to www.facebook.com/creatingmagic

The Rime of the Small, Grey, Bear
By C. Harper-Leigh
(apologies to Samuel Taylor Coleridge)

PART I

It is a small, grey, bear,
And he stoppeth one of three.
'By thy short grey hair and glittering eye,
Now wherefore stopp'st thou me?

The Llamas' doors are opened wide,
And I am next of kin;
The guests are met, the feast is set:
May'st hear the merry din.'

He holds him with his skinny paw,
'There was a bear,' quoth he.
'Hold off! unhand me, grey-haired loon!'
Eftsoons his hand dropt he.

He holds him with his glittering eye—
The Llama stood still,
And listens like a seven years' child:
The Bear hath his will.

The Llama sat on a stone:
He cannot choose but hear;
And thus spake on that small, grey, bear,
The bright-eyed Ursine pal.

'The crowd was cheered, the stupa cleared,
Merrily did we sit
Below the Temple, below the hill,
Below the pagoda top.

The Sun came up upon the left,
Out of the Temple came he!
And he shone bright, and on the right
Went down into the field.

Higher and higher every day,
Till over the hill at noon—'
The Llama here beat his dharma drum,
For he heard the loud brahma bell.

The Monks hath paced into the hall,
Orange robes hath they;
Nodding their heads before they go
The serene lotus bloom.

The Llama he beat his dharma drum,
Yet he choose but hear;
And thus spake on that small, grey, bear,
The bright-eyed Ursine pal.

And now the CLOUD-GONG came, and he
Was benevolent and strong:
He bowed with his head,
And prayed us come along.

With praying minds and furrowed brow,
As who prayed with peace and show
Still treads the shadow of E. A. Poe,
And forward bends his head,
And his books aye we read.

And now there came both mist and snow,
And it grew wondrous cold:
A Dirigible came floating by,
Its name was "Albatross".

And through the drifts the snowy clifts
Did send a dismal sheen:
Nor shapes of men nor bears we ken—
The crew was all squir'rels.

The airship was here, the airship was there,
The airship was all around:
It cracked and growled, and roared and howled,
Like noises in a swound!

At length did cross the Dirigible,
Thorough the fog it came;
As if it had been a Buddhist soul,
We hailed it in Godwin's name.

And round and round it flew.
The airship did fly with a thunder-fit;
The helmsman steered it through!
And a good south wind sprung up behind;

The Dirigible did follow,
And every day, for food or play,
Came to Red Tail's hollo!
In mist or cloud, on mast or shroud,

It perched for vespers nine;
Whiles all the night, through fog-smoke white,
Glimmered the white Moon-shine.'

'Buddha save thee, small, grey, bear!
From the fiends, that plague thee thus!—
Why look'st thou so?'—With my NERF gun
I shot the "ALBATROSS".

C. Harper-Leigh lives in a quaint village in the heart of the English countryside with a lazy cat called Sprockett, and of course George.

Before writing children's books for adults she has worked as a security guard, a receptionist for a well known publicist, plus assorted dull Admin jobs.

During this time her mind would wander off on its own, and have great adventures without her.

Tea Duelling, or, A Steampunk Sport

Photo © Steven C. Davis

Tea Mistress LM Cooke, assisted by Count Rostov, presides over the tea duelling event held at Southcart Books as part of the launch event.

Tea duelling is a fun, psychological game involving tea and biscuits. Contestants sit facing each other, hold the specified biscuit (generally, a malted milk) in the tea for a prescribed length of time, then remove and hold up the biscuit. The aim is to have the biscuit which remains intact the longest.

Tea duelling was created and developed by Geof Banyard and John Naylor. The winners of tea duelling competitions which have been officially registered (and yes, there is unregistered tea duelling!) go on to compete at The Asylum, an annual Steampunk festival held in Lincoln each August.

For a while it looked like the tea duelling competition would come down to a head to head final between Amy and Scott, our hosts and proprietors of Southcart Books, but eventually Scott (pictured) was declared the victor and awarded a winner's medal.

Photo © Craig Beas

I Saw A Yeti, Once
By C. S. Wright

Major Thompson was already well on his way to his nightly state of complete inebriation when I entered the club. Sitting in his usual spot by the fire, glass of brandy in hand, the firelight glinted off his bald spot and his cheeks were reddened, as was his bulbous nose. His eyes were half closed and his tobacco stained bushy white moustache moved slowly up and down with his breathing.

I barely noticed him, eager as I was to share my news with my friends at the next table. "I got the Nepal posting and I leave on the midday airship tomorrow!" My friends applauded and cheered and in turns clapped me on the back. It was a promotion and a great opportunity.

"Nepal?" The Major's bushy eyebrows rose. "I was in Nepal once, saw a Yeti!"
We all groaned; his stories were infamous and you could never stop him once he started. All you could do was listen until he ran out of steam.

The Major continued in his droning voice. "Back in 1876, I was a midshipman on the Airship Intrepid, survey mission as I recall. We were caught in a blizzard over the Himalayas and the infernal machine crashed. I was lucky, though I didn't think so at the time. Everyone else was killed when we hit the mountain and there I was, lying in the wreckage

31

shivering and wondering how I was going to avoid a slow, lingering death.

"Well, I got to moving a bit and gathered some extra clothes off the poor buggers who'd bought it. Never give up, eh? So I thought, head down the slope, bound to come across someone eventually. Plodded on for hours, getting weaker and colder every step."

He paused and took a gulp of brandy. "And then I saw the Yeti! It was snowing pretty hard and I thought it was a man at first until I could see it was at least seven feet tall and covered in fur. Had these big tufty ears too. Anyway, I was bloody petrified. The beast just stared at me for a moment and then turned away and strode off down the mountain. Seemed to know where he was going and I had no better plan so I followed him.

"Well, I had no idea how long I followed the Yeti for. I was cold and numb and things started to get a bit fuzzy. Eventually I realised that the creature wasn't there any more. I don't mind telling you that despair got me then, thought I really was a goner. "Lucky for me some of those Buddhist monks showed up right then. Bloody good people! Not our sort, you understand, but good people all the same. Got me back to civilisation and patched me up."

"A fine story, Major!" I said, not believing a word, and he knew it.

"Hmmph! Every word the truth. Frostbite took three of my damned fingers!" He held up his mutilated left hand and waved it at me, took a gulp of his brandy and turned to the fire, a faraway look in his eyes.

C.S. Wright is an engineer who has been writing science-fiction and fantasy short stories for over twenty years. His first novel, a thriller set in an alternative Victorian London, is due to be published in 2016 and he is also working on an anthology of steampunk short stories with a number of other writers, also due for publication in 2016. He currently works in a factory in the West Midlands and lives with his partner, Gemma, who is training to become a mad cat lady.

Raising Steam

'Raising Steam' is a music download of 22 songs, all generously donated by the bands that would have played at the 'Raising Steam' festival in Reading in September 13.

Ranging from folk to progressive rock, from funk to cabaret to musical story-telling, the compilation demonstrates the versatility and range within the Steampunk music scene.

And now – Raising Steam II is under way! Ranging from folk to horror, from progressive rock to truly alternative, the second Raising Steam compilation expands its range, capturing a snapshot of the Steampunk and Alternative music scene.

Libricide
By Adam Millard

Bishal entered his Kathmandu chamber, heart pounding with anticipation, as it always did. As the scent – an amalgamation of paper and centuries old print – reached his nostrils, he could hardly contain his excitement.

As far as the eye could see there were books. They filled shelves, shelves filled walls. In the middle of the chamber, more volumes were stacked, and though he'd taken inventory of every tome, his gaze always brushed by something he'd never seen before.

This was the *last* library in Nepal, and it was his. When the revolution began, Bishal had had enough sense to keep the books he possessed. While people wandered around, clutching and reading from computerised devices, Bishal had collected large quantities of books which people now deemed obsolete. Soon, he'd accumulated enough to line the walls of a small home. And yet people still didn't see it the way he did; they were happy, blissfully unaware of technology's fallibility.

And so Bishal continued to stockpile, and when the government decided that printed books were antediluvian, and that biblioclasm was the only sensible step, he'd bought more and more, saving them from the incinerators and county-show fires.

It was, Bishal believed, sacrilege; that these irreplaceable artefacts could be treated with such vitriol offended him, and with renewed vigour, he'd accumulated more and more. By 2030, his storage bill had eaten through the majority of his savings. Luckily, he didn't have to wait long for his premonition to pay off.

In 2033, a solar flare – the largest of its kind ever recorded – washed over earth, taking with it communications, satellites, electricity, everything that required power. Cars drifted to a halt in the middle of the road, where they remain to this day; rotting steel corpses.

By the time the flare struck, Bishal had moved into his recently-deceased grandfather's house – a large, detached residence in Sirutar – and built, eschewing his lack of architectural knowledge, a large extension on its already fathomless rear. The books were catalogued and alphabetised. Nobody, not even those close to Bishal, knew what he'd done, that he'd been obtaining these paper dinosaurs for almost two decades.

He walked through a section he'd affectionately titled, *Favourites*. This was where he kept those books to which he could return, year after year. He reached up to the second shelf, took down Melville's *Moby Dick*, and settled at a desk in the centre of the room.

The woman already seated there smiled. Bishal didn't know her, but she was very welcome. They *all* were.

"What, if you don't mind my asking, are you reading?" he said.

The lady held aloft the book in her tremulous fingers; he could see it was Heller's *Catch 22*. "I love this place," she said. "You're truly a *god* to these people."

Bishal snorted. As he glanced around the room at the connoisseurs, the academics, the scientists, all reading by gaslight, he realised that, in a strange sort of way, he *was* a god.

He read, occasionally smiling at the beautiful lady, whose name he may never discover. Bishal – not a god; just a prophet of an unsound technology, a modern-day miscarriage that humanity would never have to contend with again.

Adam Millard is the author of twenty novels, ten novellas, and more than a hundred short stories, which can be found in various collections and anthologies. Probably best known for his post-apocalyptic fiction, Adam also writes fantasy/horror for children, as well as bizarro fiction for several publishers. His "Dead" series has been the filling in a Stephen King/Bram Stoker sandwich on Amazon's bestsellers chart, and the translation rights have recently sold to German publisher, Voodoo Press.

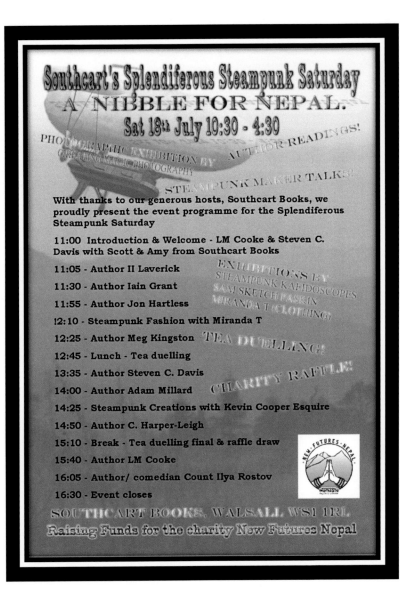

Southcart's Splendiferous Steampunk Saturday
A NIBBLE FOR NEPAL.
Sat 18th July 10:30 - 4:30

With thanks to our generous hosts, Southcart Books, we proudly present the event programme for the Splendiferous Steampunk Saturday

11:00 Introduction & Welcome - LM Cooke & Steven C. Davis with Scott & Amy from Southcart Books

11:05 - Author II Laverick

11:30 - Author Iain Grant

11:55 - Author Jon Hartless

12:10 - Steampunk Fashion with Miranda T

12:25 - Author Meg Kingston

12:45 - Lunch - Tea duelling

13:35 - Author Steven C. Davis

14:00 - Author Adam Millard

14:25 - Steampunk Creations with Kevin Cooper Esquire

14:50 - Author C. Harper-Leigh

15:10 - Break - Tea duelling final & raffle draw

15:40 - Author LM Cooke

16:05 - Author/ comedian Count Ilya Rostov

16:30 - Event closes

SOUTHCART BOOKS, WALSALL WS1 1RL
Raising Funds for the charity New Futures Nepal

Original poster for the launch event, © LM Cooke

Be careful what you wish for
By Miranda T.

Alice was bored, stuck alone in the observation cabin on night watch, five-hundred feet short of K2's summit. She'd thought being in the high-altitude research programme would be a wonderful adventure, but it had proven to be routine. She just wished something different would happen.

She heard it first; a screeching she instinctively knew was something scraping the wires holding the cabin aloft. Through the window was an impossible sight – looming from the mist and snow was an airship. A sharp ringing heralded the snapping of cables; the cabin twisted, sending Alice sliding across the now drunkenly sloping floor. Alice's quick mind knew she had but moments before the window smashed, depressurising the cabin. Hauling herself to the emergency locker and wrenching it open, she wrestled the respirator from it, pulling on the mouthpiece and goggles just before the shards of glass came crashing down around her and her ears popped as the air pressure plummeted.

Throwing the rucksack of emergency equipment onto her back, Alice launched herself towards the now useless pressure door. Opening it revealed not the enclosed rope bridge, but rather its tattered remains. The main body of the outpost was just thirty yards off but now, with no bridge and a yawning chasm below, impossible to reach.

Fighting a rising tide of panic, Alice focused on her options. She could wait for rescue from the team, but the shudders running though the cabin warned it could topple at any moment. Looking back to the shattered window, she almost cried in joy; the airship's gondola had jammed in its opening, a hatch visible with a rope dangling from it. With an agility honed by months on the mountain she scrambled up and into the airship.

Its interior was eerily lit by florescent panels, not the lamps she might have expected, illuminating steps that led upwards to the airship's bridge. Its windows were smashed and snow covered everything inside it including eight bodies, all clearly dead. Alice peered in surprise at the closest: it was encased in a rubberised suit, with metal rings at each joint and a helmet not unlike that of a diver, a brass sphere with small porthole-like windows, connected through copper pipes to oxygen bottles.

Alice was nonplussed: what use a diver on an airship? Then a flash of realisation – the airship hadn't been *rising* when it collided with the cabin, it had been *descending*. This suit was not to protect against the pressures of the deep, but the rarified atmosphere of the heavens. This must be an experimental, high-altitude airship; but what had made it crash? She looked closely at the figure – and gasped. The aeronaut's features were shrunken and twisted into a rictus of pain and fear, his skin was as pale as snow. There were punctures in the suit at neck level, but no blood around them: he had been sucked dry.

40

Alice's mind flew back four months to her ascent up the mountain. The Sherpas had talked of strange creatures that lived beyond the snowline and hunted in the thin air above the mountain. She'd dismissed it as superstition, but maybe this unlucky vessel had encountered one of these creatures. Two of the figures were holding harpoon guns, the kind with a line attached, one of which was discharged, the other still loaded. It seemed they had been prepared for something, but not prepared enough.

From behind her came a scraping sound, like something heavy and rough was pulling itself through a confined space, such as a bulkhead door. Alice didn't waste time looking behind her; she sprinted forwards, scooping up the loaded harpoon as she ran, but not to fire at the creature. Rather, her sprint continued, ending as she dived through the shattered window. Alice had an exceptional sense of direction: sailing into the void she could see, as expected, the lights of the research station below. Swinging the harpoon around, she fired. Her aim was true: it struck home into the station's wall.

Then the fall that seemed to last an eternity, heart beating fit to burst, breath held, hands wrapped around the cable, tensioning muscles for the jolt as it pulled tight, a moment of panic as the shaft seemed to pull from its anchorage, and then relief washing through her as it held.

Alice breathed again and returned her gaze to the stricken

airship. Her blood froze; silhouetted against it by the moonlight was a monstrous form. Ugly, misshaped wings stretched from it, a tentacle arching downwards. Alice was glad the swirling snow prevented her seeing any further detail. Pulling a flare from the rucksack, Alice clamped the firing cord between her teeth and pulled, aiming it into the airship's gas bag. Night was turned to day as the hydrogen ignited, engulfing the creature in a wall of flame. The ruined airship hung for a second and then began to fall, tumbling down the mountainside trailing tendrils of fire.

"Alice! Are you there?" Looking up, she could see an open hatch with figures leaning from it.

"Down here!" she shouted weakly. Now all she had to do was explain what the hell happened.

I became interested in creating Steampunk clothing through 'period' dressing (principally Victorian and 1940s/50s), which itself was an outcome of being being attracted to the elegance of these era's styles and and a general fascination with the history of those times. However, Steampunk gives much greater latitude in one's designs, re-imagining a past that never was and merrily cherry-picking aspects from different time periods and adding twists of one's own within the rich backdrop of the Steampunk aesthetic. I also enjoy writing, particularly 'alternate-history' storylines, which fits in nicely with the Steampunk genre.

"The windy valley", the Annapurnas, Nepal 2004.

Top Gear
By Keith Errington

The Yeti smiled and pointed. Although perhaps 'smile' was a tad optimistic for the lop-sided grin the creature painfully created on its face.

Clarkson shook his head and tutted. "Snowball here says that way." He shouted above the noise of the machines.

"Well, we should respect local knowledge." May shouted back, running his hand through his smut-ridden hair.

They both turned to Hammond who was standing next to his machine grinning inanely; a look immortalised in countless engravings in the Illustrated London News.

"Let's go!" shouted Clarkson and climbed the rungs up to the seat of his steam walker. A huge red beast, made by the Italian company of Farriro, it was by far the fastest of the three machines, on a flat, smooth road, it could manage an almost unbelievable 12 miles per hour!

May's walker was almost as big, and certainly more brutal in appearance, made by the German company of Fabrik Mechanische, his "Dampf männlich" was efficient but slow.

Then off to the left was a contraption that looked like a spherical cage covered in spikes. Slung within was a small steam engine and a canvas chair. This was Hammond's conveyance, a machine which had inevitably been nicknamed by the team, "the Hamster Wheel". Made by the Wallace Company of Burton, based on a design by

Heath Robinson, it often struggled on any surface not entirely horizontal.

"To Everest!" Shouted Clarkson dramatically.

Of course, the truth of the matter was, they were nowhere near Everest, they were attempting one of the much smaller, gentler foothills on the edge of Nepal's most famous mountain chain. But their publisher knew that for the purposes of the serialised accounts, any snow covered bump would do, as long as readers were told it was Everest, they would believe it was Everest.

With a massive expulsion of steam and a thunderous crescendo of noise the three machines set off again, 'up' the ragged path. Despite the noise and engine horsepower, the native guides and Snowball had no problems keeping up, at times even pausing to let the mechanical contrivances negotiate a small stone or a particularly large tuft of grass. The two writers followed on pack ponies that were being led in the terrible trio's wake.

Inevitably it was Hammond who dropped out first, a deer startled by the unfamiliar noise had run in entirely the wrong direction and Hammond had been forced to violently swerve to avoid it. The Wallace was manifestly incapable of such a manoeuvre and spiralled sideways out of control down a slope, and, eventually, out of sight.

Once the writers had stopped laughing they immediately caused a halt to the percussive procession to interview May and Clarkson about the temporary loss of their teammate.

Finally they got going again having covered a magnificent 80 yards since the last stop. The Italian machine was the next to bow out: a piston blew as Clarkson pressed it forward at top speed. Nuts, bolts and a wide range of unidentified metal shrapnel shot out of the front of the machine, with some missing Clarkson's head by a few inches. Unfortunately, those inches were southwards and to the left, breaking Clarkson's arm and rendering him unable to carry on. "It's my throttle arm you see," he explained to the nodding writers.

So May carried on, the lone German engine slowly, but steadily, eating up the inches.

It was all going so well, when, sixty feet from the 'summit' a strand of May's hair caught in one of the männlich's moving parts and he was slung from his seat with some force and strewn across the mountain like a rag doll. The writers rushed over to him as he dusted himself off.

"I'm fine," he blustered, clearly shaken by the experience.

But then, they all turned their eyes back to the path as Snowball pointed once again, this time with his furry jaw dropped. The indefatigable, relentless German machine was carrying on up the path all by itself, much faster now it was one May lighter. It reached the summit. And kept going. And as the sun went down over the Himalayas they watched as small puffs of steam gave clues as to its passage across Nepal, heading, almost inevitably, for Everest itself.

Keith Errington is a blogger, copywriter, comedy writer, food lover, steampunk and comedian. From winning his first short story competition at the age of very young – he knew it was his destiny to be a poor and penniless writer.

Fortunately, fate intervened and he currently makes a reasonable living in marketing. He lives in the Midlands with his three computers and a dalek.

The launch event at Southcart Books, 18th July 2015

Photo © Craig Beas

C. Harper-Leigh reading from her work. Photo © LM Cooke

Tea duelling! Photo © Craig Beas

Adam Millard © Craig Beas   Kev Cooper © Steven C. Davis

Photo © Steven C. Davis

A Flower Blossoms
By Steven C. Davis

Suni wrinkled her nose. The mountain air was acidic, burning, not typical. She coughed, spitting out tobacco. The village looked peaceful. Calm. But Anita's husband was gone, run off with another man; Maya's husband would never work again, what with his broken leg, and their three children would be fortunate to survive. The air shivered like a heat haze. But the air was cool, smelling of burning. Suni rubbed her hands together. She had been to Kathmandu once, seen the fear and smelled it also, and it was no comparison – ever – for her village.

Suni removed the small packet from where she had tucked it into her belt. A handful of seeds. A scattering of hope. It was all she could afford. The plants clung tightly to the slopes, but the wind scoured, the winter was bitter and the monsoon drowned many. Still, without the seeds –

Suni lifted her head. Goose bumps ran up her arms. She could feel every hair on her head, and every layer of clothing felt simultaneously too tight and too loose. Her mouth was dry. She stretched her hand out to touch the mani wall – and felt it in her stomach.

The earth – capsized. It had never felt anything like this when she had had a husband. Not when her child had been born. She had never felt anything like this before, and she'd been trapped by monsoon waters, and been in the village when Maoists had paid them a visit.

She was falling, and flying, simultaneously. It was an exhilarating and terrifying experience. The world was joyously alive, ablaze with movement and sound and everything bright, oh so bright.

Sagarmatha was rippling. She'd seen a Westerner running once. Their blonde hair had rippled and Suni had, for a moment, wondered what it would be like to be that Westerner, with their blonde hair and their lack of care.

The mani stones were coming apart. A splinter of red stone, red as the Sandhus' adorned themselves when seeking tourists, seeking attention. Red as the dress she had once worn when she was a child.

The seeds flew from her hand. That was – well, that was her life. No husband, no child. Without a crop to sell or to trade, she had no one to support her. Kathmandu beckoned but she'd smelled it once before and the mountain was her home.

Suni shuddered at the thought. Her people were mountain people. Her parents had never left the village, never, fortunately, smelled the future.

There was a moment – she had cut her leg badly as a child, and had stared at it in surprise for an instant, before screaming.

There was a moment – when she had helped Amil deliver her baby and the world had seemed rich and full of promise.

There was a moment – and it stretched out into the forever.

And then there was – no more.

And in the valley down below, a flower blossomed.

52

Steven C. Davis is the author of 'Cornix Sinistra' and 'Armageddon Angel', which are works of intersecting alternate-earths' fiction, set around an independent bookshop. He is the co-author of 'The Heart's Cog Imperative', (with S. J. Stewart), book 1 of which has recently been published, and has a poetry collection, 'Sorrow Works'.

He is the host of the Gothic, Alternative, Steampunk and Progressive web radio show (with LM Cooke) which goes out Thursday evenings on Blast 1386 between 8 and 11pm. In between working full time and sleeping, he also bakes fiendishly rich chocolate cakes. Find out more at www.tenebroustexts.com

Our hosts for the event – Southcart Books!

Hosted by Scott and Amy Carter, Southcart Books is the only independent bookshop in the Walsall area. They specialise in sci-fi, horror, fantasy and non-fantasy, plus vintage and antique books and comics.

Southcart Books hold regular events, encouraging local (and not so local!) authors to get involved, actively supporting them by carrying their works.

With their Steampunk lounge full of mementoes from previous events and curios both for sale and to be admired, Southcart Books is well worth a trip if you're in the area.

They can also be found online, on facebook, ebay and amazon (search for Southcart Books).

Where The Poppies Bloom
By James Josiah

The man who has lived forever looks across the battlefield, turns to Death and says, "I remember when all of this will be fields."

"You know I hate it when you do that," says Death, frustration dripping off every word.

"Do what?" He replies, barely concealing the grin that was spreading across his face.

"Mix your tenses. You can not remember that which has not yet happened."

"But I have seen it. I have seen it all. I saw all of this while man was discovering fire. I witnessed the war after this one while they were still a single cell. You should know, you have been there through it all."

While it is true that Death has been there at each and every step the human race has taken so far and will remain by its side until the bitter end, time itself was something that Death has never bothered to trouble himself with.

Humans like to think themselves as the most intelligent things on the planet. But time is a man made product and only limits our existence. Animals don't bother themselves with it. While the sheep knows when to breed so her lambs are born in spring, she doesn't trouble herself with the concept of Tuesdays.

It was Death's turn to take in the destruction that lay before them. If he could he would have sighed at the futility of it all. The dead lay in various states of dismemberment and decay as far as the eye could see. He thought to himself that it was a jolly good thing he didn't believe in time as this would take him ages to clean up.

The little joke makes him titter and he starts to tell it to the man who has lived forever. Before he can reach the punchline the man stops him by saying, "I've already heard that one, you tell it to me when the bombs fall."

"That's the problem with you," snaps Death, "you bloody well think you know everything!"

Sensing the change in mood the eternal being apologises, "it is a blessing and a curse and for what it's worth I am sorry. It's a good joke. Tell it me again and I promise I'll laugh."

"It's too late now, the moment has passed, I was only trying to lighten the mood," replies Death grumpily.

"How can the moment pass – if you don't believe in time?"

"It's a figure of speech!" Seethed Death. "For an almighty being you aren't very wise."

"Wisdom is a matter of perspective. Now come on, you harvest the dead and I'll sow the seeds. Who knows maybe this time they'll see the poppies and the errors of their ways."

"That's what I like about you," says Death, "you've seen it all and you're still an optimist."

James Josiah is an author, editor and a male human being. His debut novel Days of Madness was released last year and people seemed to quite like it. His latest offering, C90, a tale of love, loss and music was released in the autumn. He likes the silly things in life, piña coladas and getting caught in the rain. He dislikes talking about himself in the third person.

GASP Radio

Broadcasting online through Blast 1386 on Thursday evenings between 8 and 11pm, repeated on Saturday's from 7 until 10am, GASP radio (that's Gothic, Alternative, Steampunk and Progressive) is hosted by Steven C. Davis and LM Cooke and plays a varied mix of the above, as well as carnival, folk, metal, cabaret and music hall. Join the weekly facebook events for the full experience!

www.facebook.com/GASPradioshow
www.mixcloud.com/stevencdavis10
GASP@Blast1386.com

Snow, Sun, Steam
By LM Cooke

When we reached the rest station the sun was setting and temperatures were dropping. I surveyed the expensive clockwork yaks. The oil in their joints was thickening; soon they would seize up entirely. It was time to unload them, transfer their packages onto the Sherpas.

The Sherpas were not happy at this: my assistant's Nepalese had been insufficient to explain that this was likely. Nevertheless, as the sun rose over the shelters the next morning we left the clockwork creatures behind and trekked on into the hills.

We saw no sign of our quarry on that day, nor the next, nor next. No spoor, no tracks. I began to doubt my own beliefs. Perhaps we sought a myth rather than monster. Perhaps there was nothing out here in these endless Himalayan ranges but snow and more snow. I kept my thoughts to myself, not wanting our guides to question me. My assistant looked increasingly pinch-faced and miserable. Admittedly, the camera he was carrying was heavy; a shame the Sherpas were already so burdened.

On the fifth day, a blizzard blew up from nowhere. We plodded on grimly until forced to make halt against a rocky outcrop and seek shelter from the storm. Somehow our guides made a fire and kept it burning behind our tarpaulins, while the wind howled and growled outside.

In the dead of the night I awoke. The wind had dropped and the blizzard cleared and the star-filled sky was vast and close when I peered out of our shelter. In the moonlight I finally saw the first evidence that what we sought was not a myth. Footprints – huge, unearthly footprints in the snow around our shelter.

I shook my assistant awake, motioned for him to join me with the camera, praying the moonlight would hold. I retrieved my Helios and Wesson, the new purpose-bought sun-ray-gun I had obtained before I left for Nepal. The Sherpas muttered and shook their heads as we foolish Westerners ventured outside, following the tracks leading away from our shelter. The torch shook in my assistant's hand as we trekked further into the hills, into the snow. Until finally the tracks stopped at a hollow. Our quarry was inside.

I instructed my assistant to set up the camera. I planned to creep around behind and scare the monster out while my assistant took the daguerrotype. Carefully I inched my way around the hollow then leaped into it, firing the Helios. The camera flash went off with a pop!

Unfortunately, I had not considered that the yeti, my abominable snowman, might actually be made from snow. My assistant's filmic endeavours captured only a cloud of steam as the sunrays from my gun evaporated our quarry into harmless water. When I searched the lair, all that remained were two chunks of coal-like, scorched rock and a random charred carrot, poor return for my trophy wall.

I have ordered a Winchester Frigidaire freeze-ray gun. I will be back. Soon.

LM Cooke writes dark fantasy and science fiction, influenced by authors like Tanith Lee and JRR Tolkien. She is author of Steampunk series 'The Automata Wars'. She has contributed short stories to various compilations, including the first three volumes of 'The Asylum Chronicles' Steampunk anthologies, published through The Last Line.

LM Cooke is also vocalist in the band Crimson Clocks and co-host on the GASP (Gothic, Alternative, Steampunk, Progressive) radio show on Blast 1386. In her spare time she plots galactic domination, while pandering to an overindulged feline. Find out more at www.LMCooke.com

Steampunk How To Paint a Gun
By Kev Cooper (Steampunk Relics)

One of the easiest "Steampunk makes" is a gun modification, or even simpler a makeover paint job. Nerf guns are a firm favourite to work with but if it's your first attempt then use something cheap like a water pistol. There are some great ray guns around. Have a look in discount shops for water pistols and charity shops for old Nerf guns and other interesting toy guns, pirate flintlocks for instance.

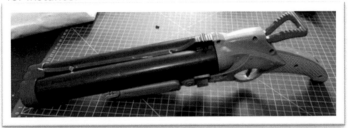

Photo © Kev Cooper

Step one, remove all of the seams and the "made in china" use a sharp knife blade or a file or fine abrasive paper. It's not really necessary to dismantle the gun if it's a simple one like a water pistol. Next rub down the whole gun with fine steel wool. Now remove all of the dust and give the gun a coat of matt black acrylic spray paint. Nothing expensive, look around the discount shops. If you haven't got a garage or shed to paint in you'll have to wait for a dry day and work outside. If you're indoors wear a mask. See the instructions on the can for drying times; it's usually pretty quick for acrylic paint.

Now you can start painting the details in the colours of your choice. Acrylic paints are best for this, the ones from Games Workshop are ideal but the snap tops they use these days are not good, they dry up quite quickly if not used. This is one time when cheap paints are not good enough. But as you'll see you'll have enough to paint a few guns. We're going to use the "dry brush" technique for this part, if you're painting large areas of a big gun then use a big soft brush about an inch across. Obviously for smaller details you'll need smaller brushes, again not expensive ones; you'll quickly ruin your best water colour brushes.

Take the colour of choice and stir it up, cocktail sticks are handy, put a very small amount of paint on the tip of the brush bristles, what you remove from the cocktail stick is more than enough, now brush it across a sheet of newspaper, remove almost all of the paint then carefully brush the part of the gun you're working on. If you see brush marks appear then you have too much paint on the brush. You want to see barely any paint appear on the gun, keep repeating until you have the effect you like, it's amazing how it makes the texture of the plastic pop out even though it looked smooth before. It can really look like metal rather than plastic. Repeat the process on all the parts of the gun. That's it; it's simple but very effective. You can always add stuff to the gun, bit of wire, switches, anything you find that looks good. You can give the finished gun a spray coat of clear lacquer to help protect the paint from wear and tear. Matt lacquer looks best.

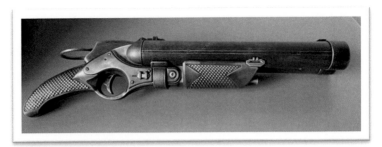

Photo © Kev Cooper

You can see more of Kev's amazing work at www.steampunkrelics.co.uk

Photo © Steven C. Davis

The man in the white coat
***From* 'the diary of the dark detective'**
By Stu Tovell

I took the cab from my office to Alexandra Palace where the French airship Swan Song was waiting for me.
I was greeted by Captain Cremon and his pet monkey, Everett.

Cremon informed me that we were to make a quick stop in Kathmandu, a man called Thapa wanted to meet me on an urgent matter.

My cabin was small but comfortable; there was Absinthe and cigars and a rather attractive hostess who said she would keep me company on this short journey.

Upon arrival, I met up with Thapa who handed me a small box with some writing on it.

"Do you recognise the writing Miss Noir?" he said this with some enthusiasm as if he already knew my answer.
"Is it Kusunda?"
He smiled and went on to explain.
"Years ago there was an attempt to climb K2, lead by Albert Crawley, all but one of his team were found dead. We searched for weeks but could not find him.
Other climbers said they had seen a large bearded man dressed in white screaming and then just seemed to vanish, since then we have had other similar reports.

One expedition returned with this box covered in blood saying that they had fought off the man and taken it from him before he disappeared."

I took another look at the box, the words inscribed simply said the door that loops, I had heard of such boxes before.
Many great men had written of it, often confusing it for something more spiritual, some scientific types had even put forward ideas of parallel worlds or concepts of time travel.

In many ways Blake, DeRais and Dee had been on the right track, but it was the Benedictine monk Herman the Recluse who solved the puzzle.
He had discovered that there were doorways throughout the world that allowed you to access a point in time, but in order to avoid being thrown into a loop you must have the means to control the path.
He spent many years working on a key, until finding the correct configuration.
It was a simple design of two overlapping circles with a line running through the middle.
A fellow Detective, with a reputation as dark as my own, had shown me the original manuscript.
He owned one of the keys which had been turned into a small silver ring.
I did my best to explain things to Thapa; he listened and then said:

"Thank you, Miss Noir, you have been most helpful, but what of this man in white?"

I shook my head.
"Without the key, he is forever stuck in that loop and will appear from time to time forever more, his own fault but not surprising, that was always his problem, far too impatient, instead of trying to learn more first he just went straight in without thinking.
He should never have opened that box, yet he did."

Stu Tovell was born in the 1960's, at a slight angle to the universe. Went on to be a musician in the late 1970's and then kept going. Releasing with various bands a number of albums and singles up to 2010.The writing started after working as a researcher compiling discographies and background information in the mid 1980's. He is credited in over 50 published books. Nowadays better known as the creator of the surreal, twisted and absinthe soaked world of the Dark Detective, appearing in various short stories and the novella The Blood Stained Mask.

The peak of the Thorong-La pass, Annapurnas, Nepal, 2006

A wall of mani stones, said to protect a village.

The Hope Centre 2006

The Englishman who went up a Mountain and came down a hill
By Adrian Middleton

The mountain loomed overhead.

"Trees grow at that altitude?" Basil Upton Fosdyke asked.

"The roots are down here," said Captain Flyte. "Only the top is up there."

"Where? I'm sure I'd have heard about a tree that big. Or seen it."

"It's *inside* the mountain." Augustus Flyte covered his rime-frosted beard, pulling down his goggles. "Follow me."

Fosdyke and the Sherpa escort followed, traipsing along snowy slopes for 1000 metres until flapping flags and a cluster of rock-weighted tents emerged, set against a sheer cliff sheltering them from the wind. Poking through a rocky fissure, the engineer spied a tuberous protuberance. Presumably one of the aforementioned roots.

"That's a root? It's *ginormous*."

It was as wide as a London omnibus and much taller. Basil wondered if his steam-powered Chipper was the best tool for the job. It tested well on giant redwoods, but this...?

"This is the widest of several roots, providing the straightest path through the mountain."

"Couldn't you just bore into it? My Chipper could take weeks."

"We only need to reach its heart — where the sap flows. Then we'll poison it. Dead wood is easier to remove. Wood-chipping won't destabilize like explosions and vibrating rock will."

#

After some minutes the equipment was unpacked and Fosdyke's patented Chipper Chipper was assembled. The steam generator was the largest component. The boring screw came a close second. Strapping on the unit, Basil wondered how long it would last before breaking down. Pulling on padded gloves, he adjusted his oxygen mask. Pressed firmly against his chest, the vibrations would shatter his bones without the kinetic absorbers he had engineered. *I'm brilliant*, he told himself.

"The starter cable is on the generator," he explained. "You need to grip hard and pull firmly. Can't afford to flood the engine."

"Righto," said Flyte.

Basil squared up to the thick, pale wood.

Vrrrrmmmm-vrmmmmmmmmmmm.

#

The wood soon became balsa-like. Progress was quicker than expected and he soon reached the centre of the root, disappearing from sight. Augustus Flyte listened intently as the sound of the Chipper faded. His Sherpas swept aside the wood-chips chipped by the Chipper Chipper. The wind scattering them faster than they could be gathered. *Soon,* he grinned, *the world's highest copper mine will be open for business.*

Deep inside the mountain's belly sap burst forth. The Chipper slipped, piercing the wood and striking rock. Sparks flew as the blades halted, fragmenting as the rock resisted the attack.

"Lawks!" Basil cursed, pulling the fast-release cord. He was carried downwards by the running sap. Like riding a water flue he approached the base of the tree.

"Geronimooooooo!"

#

The Captain witnessed the inevitable. Vibrations loosened snow and ice. The mountain cracked apart.

"Avalanche!" Flyte fled, shooing the Sherpas away. He should, perhaps, have shouted *"rockslide!"*

Basil popped out like a cork, shooting above the fleeing party as the mountain fell apart. Several minutes later the cloud of rocks settled, leaving behind a pile of rubble or — based on its new height and shape — a hill.

Adrian Middleton is a former civil servant and policy advisor on broadband and digital content. He shares his time between Birmingham and Wales, and is the founding director of Fringeworks Ltd.

Adrian's life in publishing began as a prolific fanzine editor, producing some 300 issues in the early 1990s. These included Neutron Flow, Fowling Piece (a fiction fanzine) and Rumours. His first book was Shelf Life, an anthology published in memory of his friend Craig Hinton. He then spent several years writing strategies and policy documents for the government.

He has contributed to Ain't No Sanity Clause and Grimm & Grimmer and NeaDNAthal, although most of his work is pseudonymous. He has also developed several series bibles for the company, with various works under development. He is editor of Weird Tails and the Moriarty Paradigm series, for which he has written a number of stories.

Heart's Cog Designs by S. J. Stewart

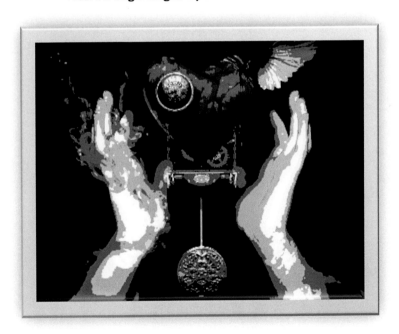

'The Heart's Cog' © S. J. Stewart

In addition to being an artist, S. J. Stewart is also the co-author of 'The Heart's Cog Imperative', published by Tenebrous Texts.

'Bilbette', specially commissioned piece © S. J. Stewart

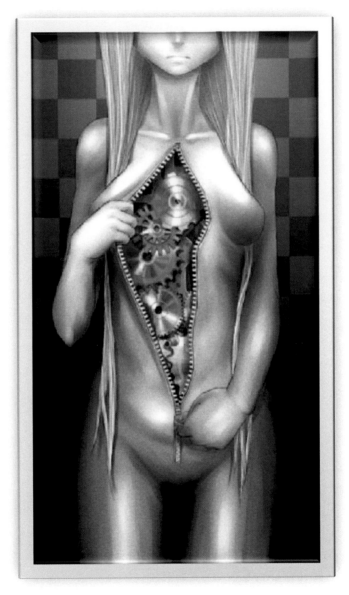

'The Clockwork Girl' © S. J. Stewart

The Mechanical Yak Attack
By Jon Hartless

"You all know the greatest problem we have faced since our forced relocation to Tibet?" asked Professor Smyth to his family, glossing over the small matter of his accidently blowing up half of London with his experimental Death Ray. "Of course, dear," replied his wife, Rosalie. "It's the untidy way those horrid yaks wander all over our land."

"And the lack of sport," muttered his daughter, Clara, hefting her favourite automated laser-sighted multi-projectile launcher. "I've had nothing to shoot at for weeks except for those bloody yaks."

"I know, dear," sympathised her mother. "And the way those wretched monks complain just because we killed one or two of their yaks to make these fine cloaks and gloves. And shoes. And cups, saucers, plates, cutlery, chairs, and tables. Just the essentials of life. And jewellery. And decorations. And umbrella stands."

"It's not as if we get any pleasure from it," protested Clara. "I mean, the stupid things just stand there, looking at you. They don't even run when you give them a mild zap with a laser stick. We'd get more sport by shooting at the monks, if you ask me. At least they'd provide a faster target."

"Now, now, my dear," smiled Smyth in paternal approval. "They are men of the cloth, even if it is the wrong cloth, as I tried to explain to their abbot when I said I would heed his words the day he stops being a godless Buddhist and becomes a proper Church of England vicar. Now, where was I?"

"The yak problem?"

"Yes, indeed. My dears, I think I have solved it. Behold!" Smyth opened a door and revealed several long-haired bovids in his laboratory.

"Oh, marvellous, more bloody yaks," muttered Clara.

"No! Well, yes, but not just yaks, for these are mechanical attack yaks! Designed to repel the real thing. I shall activate the herd and henceforth we can walk our land without having the view ruined by these revolting creatures." Smyth pressed a button on his control box and the mechanical figures jerked. A faint ticking and hissing could be heard as small steam generators turned various clockwork gears in each beast.

"Why are their eyes glowing red?" asked Clara.

"Ah, now that means they are in 'kill mode'. They have detected a real yak and are about to deal with it."

"But there are no yaks in here," said Rosalie, nervously. "Are they going to attack us?"

"Of course not, they are programmed to protect us – ARGH!"

A short laser beam erupted from the lead yak's left nostril, lightly toasting the professor.

"It's the yak fur we're wearing," exclaimed Clara in horror. "They can't distinguish between us and real yaks! They can't even distinguish between *themselves* and real yaks," she added as the herd turned on itself. Laser beams blasted off in several directions.

"How do we stop them from killing us?"

"Oh, um, I think, yes, er, strip! Strip for your lives!"

"Too late!" wailed Clara as she accelerated to the door, the herd of rampaging mechanical yaks at her heels. "It's every yak for himself!"

Jon Hartless was born in the 1970s and is the author of several novels and novellas, some written under his own name, some under the identities of Barnabas Corbin, Arabella Wyatt and Ora le Brocq, the latter being for adults only.
Jon's fiction under his Arabella Wyatt pseudonym include the Lady Mechatronic romance/steampunk/pirate series and Pandora, a young adult supernatural tale inspired by Greek myth, the intolerance of Mary Whitehouse, and the cult TV show The Prisoner.
His latest work under the Arabella name is The Horror of Kuchisake-Onna, in which domestic abuse is explored via the infamous Japanese urban legend of the slit-mouthed woman.

Available from Tenebrous Texts:

Jacaranda owns her own bookshop. But it's not just any bookshop: it leads into alternate versions of her home town. When she discovers her husband comes from an alternate reality, it's only the first of many revelations.

'Woods and Wales' is an internationally respected bookshop at the heart of the Royal British Empire. But when the Empire arrest the owners, there are unexpected ramifications.

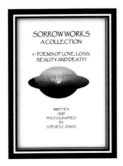

21 poems, written and photographed by Steven C. Davis, about love, loss, beauty and death.

Available from www.etsy.com/uk/shop/TenebrousTexts

Living Goddess
By Danielle Miller

The travellers sat around a shared campfire on a chilly night in Ladakh. They had shared songs and stories, and one of the merchants had just told a tall tale of his escapades.

"Tell me; have you ever heard of the Kumari-Devi, the Living Goddess of Kathmandu?" asked the elderly Pandit Shah.

"It is a belief of the Nepali that a specially chosen girl becomes the Goddess until she bleeds, then becomes mortal again and another is chosen. Thus has it been for many ages, and I would tell you of the daughter of Kuldeep who became Goddess."

"It was before the time of my birth that a new Devi needed to be found, and the people brought their young daughters to the priests in the hope that she might be chosen. The girls were examined and only those with perfection of features could be considered. She must have a horoscope which showed divinity, and be blessed with the voice and demeanour to be Goddess. Many came, and many were turned away. Only a few remained, and then Kuldeep arrived to present Sangita, his daughter.

"She was about six years of age, well formed and graceful. Her skin was light, as was her voice. After consulting her near perfect horoscope, and watching her dance and sing, the priests were impressed and she moved on to the next stage.

"The girls were then led into a dark room. Smoke, thunderflashes and dancers in demon costumes all threatened them. Some cried, some screamed, some ran. All except Sangita who stood calmly and did not flinch. The priests declared that they had found their Goddess, and Sangita was installed as Kumari-Devi.

"She proved to be untiring, always cheerful and wise beyond her years. People flocked from far and wide to worship and be blessed by the Goddess, and she won the hearts of all. Her only real demand was that her Father be allowed to visit her once per week without fail.

"It had been two years since her selection, and the Goddess remained unchanged. People marvelled at this, but she was the Kumari-Devi? Then a strange event occurred; Kuldeep became ill and could not visit for over a month. After the second week, the Goddess entered a trance from which she did not rise. She was not breathing, and all feared that their beloved Devi had ascended to heaven. A deputation of priests went to the remote house where Kuldeep lived, and almost dragged the sick man from his bed to try and raise her.

"He was taken into her chamber and some time later the Goddess came out dancing and singing to greet her followers. She stated that she had been communing with heaven in her trance, but that she was returned to them.

"All was well for another ten years, and the Goddess changed not one bit. But then Kuldeep died suddenly, and again she went into a trance shortly after. This time she did not return, and eventually the priests enshrined her undecaying body before choosing a new Goddess.

"But I myself had witnessed the Goddess as a young man visiting Kathmandu, and later I visited the lonely house where Kuldeep had lived, and found there a strange key. Then stealthily I entered her shrine and examined the unchanged body of Sangita. I found an unusual hole on her back – and the key fitted into it. Turning it a few times, she sprung to life and asked for her Father. I discoursed with her for a little while before she returned to her trance state, then I left."

Holding forth an unusual key on a chain around his neck, Pandit Shah continued. "Kuldeep was a man of talent, and ahead of his time, brothers!"

Danielle Miller is a complex puzzle of multiple personas that arose in rural Essex during the 1960s. Raised in seclusion by mechanics before running away to London in the 80s. Then spending several years travelling the world (although not yet Nepal), she eventually settled in Cornwall. With a career so far including disciplines as diverse as cucumber training, burlesque dancing and surgery, she is a polymath, cabaret performer and writer; but this is her first published work under this name.

Steampunk on a Shoestring
By Miranda T.

Making Steampunk clothing is a wonderful outlet for one's steam-driven creativity, but with a bit of careful planning needn't be a costly one.

Charity shops, sale-rails and the back of the wardrobe can all provide the basis for an outfit. Here a bustier-style 'undie' and a frilly wrap (brought in the sales) have been conjoined (with the wrap as a bustle skirt), finished off with an edging of chiffon scarf from the aforementioned wardrobe.

The second example is a circle skirt, again a sale item, with the material from its sides pulled back and up, then tacked into place to give a bustle. The dress is a charity shop find; clearly gothic style, but steamed up by the addition of chains and leather straps from an old handbag.

A stash of recycled items, such as cording, bows and ribbons, is a must, and packaging can be repurposed too. The fascinator shown has a crisp tube at its centre, whilst the hat's brim and top are fabricated from the oval lid of a chocolate box; recycled stiff card completes their structures. Both are covered with offcuts of material and adorned by recycled bits of cord, a few charity shop items and some inexpensive wool.

Garments can be made from scratch quite cheaply too. This jacket was designed to keep out cold winter winds and fit over a full bustle or crinoline. Its outer material is a deeply piled blanket bought from a supermarket for a very reasonable price, and the lining was from a charity shop duvet. Its pattern pieces were cherry-picked from my collection of patterns (end of stock ones can be very cheap), one giving the sleeves, another the bodice, etc. They were transferred onto baking parchment and adjusted to fit one another. One little tip here – make up the lining first to check for size, as any mistakes can be easily hidden.

The crinoline is also from a pre-loved duvet. It is just a set of long, thin rectangles, each longer than its predecessor, gathered at the join to make a casing for a hoop which is made from thin plastic pipe as used for plumbing – a lot cheaper and easier to obtain than lengths of spring steel.

And sometimes it's fun to make something a bit silly. The final picture is of my 'parasol skirt', made from recycled umbrella spokes attached to an elasticated belt and covered with netting and lace. It gives a very wide (if rather short) skirt, as hoops would, but it can be folded down for packing.

Just Our Luck
By I. I. Laverick

"I don't think we deserve this." The time traveller grumbled, as she and her companion trudged through the jagged landscape, barely a fraction into the vast mountains and both of them still dressed for Victorian England.

"Maxine, we meddled in the Ripper case, crashed the Great Exhibition, and finished *The Mystery of Edwin Drood*. It must have taken ten paradoxes to clear up our fine mess." Celeste frowned, using her one mechanical arm to pull herself up on to another rock.

"We're time travellers, it's an occupational hazard." Maxine protested, "it hardly warrants a trip to old Nepal to catch an unspecified havoc-wreaking beastie."

"Well, *the powers that be* clearly disagree." Celeste concluded, lifting her skirts to climb, "And if *I* were a havoc-wreaking beastie, this is where I would go."

"*Naturally.* Still, it could be worse. They could have sent you to the Boston Tea Party again." Maxine grinned.

Celeste grumbled something about sacrilege and wasting tea.

For a while, the pair began to wonder if they were even in the right place – until they found themselves *corrected*.

Celeste's mechanical arm began the ordeal by promptly whacking Maxine.

"Ouch! Will you watch where you're swinging that!?" Maxine snapped, rubbing her bruised shoulder.

"It's not my fault." Celeste retorted, but suddenly realised they had *bigger* problems. "Haven't we seen that rock before?"

Maxine frowned, "Only twice. You realise we're going around in circles?"

Confused, Celeste looked down at the compass in her brass palm. "Oh dear," she uttered. As if it knew they'd caught on, it was now spinning uselessly. "Now what do we do?"

Maxine thought for a moment, but her expression changed to suspicion when she felt the flying machine packed away on her back jolt. "That can't be goo-"

Before she could finish, two great clockwork wings snapped out and thwacked Celeste over the head.

"Oww," She murmured, her head spinning. For several moments, she saw the bizarre and disturbing sight of *several* Maxines frowning.

"This bad luck is beyond even our standards!" Celeste exclaimed, dodging as her clockwork arm turned on its owner. She had to sit on the thing to keep it down.

Maxine thought for a moment. "Bad luck," she murmured, "bad luck – Nepal – beasties – AHA!"

Her companion raised her eyebrows.

"Celeste, set your pistol to 'net'" Maxine whispered, taking out a clockwork lantern and winding it up.

Celeste obeyed, puzzled, "Why?"

"Because there is a Khyah right behind you." Maxine hissed. "And it's been following us."

On three, they turned around, and a black, ape like creature was caught writhing in Celeste's net.

"Oh my!" Celeste exclaimed.

"I studied these on my last visit here." Maxine explained animatedly, "The black one brings bad luck on encounter-"

"Max…" Celeste tried to interject.

"I didn't believe they existed, it's truly fascinating to see one up close."

"Maxine –"

"– And I should have realised what we were dealing with, though I am rusty on my Nepalese mythology –"

"MAXINE!"

Maxine sighed. "There's a big one behind me, isn't there?"

Celeste narrowed her eyes.

"What do you think?"

I. I. Laverick resides in the glamorous land of the West Midlands, with a glitchy time travelling pocket watch and a serious dependence on tea. She can usually be found haunting a tea emporium or a book shop, and identified by her shameless sense of style. Miss Laverick is the proud author of one full length self-published novel Dead Night, and writes in between her studies to become an illustrator and animator. She otherwise prides herself most in being wanted dead or alive by seven monarchs, ten Lords and a Count.

Clockwise from top left: Everest region, Nepal, 2011; Everest region; Festival of Lights, Kathmandu; and Boudhanath Stupa, Kathmandu

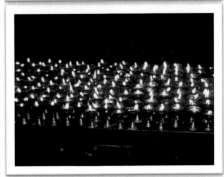

High Mission to Sagarmāthā
By A. Stuart Williams

The wind howled like the stressed-out steam turbines aft as *Turbinia* sliced through it at four hundred air-knots, high above the cloud-sea enshrouding the mighty Himalayas.

Only the hundred-foot prototype gravship's blade-like profile stopped it being ripped apart at these speeds. Some way behind, the stubbier HMGS *Viper* and *Cobra*, having a harder time of it, struggled to keep up. The Imperial Air Navy's first aerial torpedo destroyers streamlining was incomplete, and the rescue gondolas hastily attached to their flanks made things worse.

Flight-Captain Sidney Webster ('Pebbler' to his friends, after his cheerily-freckled cheeks) called back to his navigator, Harry Andrews.

"How's the course, Andrews? See any landmarks yet?"

Andrews, a second lieutenant seconded to the Tesla-Parsons Project from the Imperial Naval Academy, Greenwich two years ago, was one of the first officers of the new Combined Air Service. Eyes screwed tight to the binocular sighting 'scope at the front of the navigation dome, he peered beyond the limit of his famously sharp eyes.

There was little to see at first, but then, curving up over the horizon, a tiny, dark point appeared, rapidly looming larger now. It could be just one thing.

"Target sighted, sir! There's only one mountain that high!"

"Sagarmāthā —" A sigh of relief escaped the lips of the small, smartly-uniformed Nepalese man standing at Webster's shoulder.

"Mount Everest —" hissed the Empire's top pilot through clenched teeth.

"Ready your men, Jemadar!" Pebbler nodded to the soldier, smiling. A grateful nod replied.

Jangia Thapa's eyes lit up. Now was their chance. He signalled his fellow Gurkhas, strapped into fifteen iron seats hastily bolted in the rear of the cabin. As always, they were ready for anything, but tightened their snowsuits, checked webbing and secured their kukhuris anyway.

Bare minutes later, they were hovering above the peak of Everest, *Turbinia's* turbo-fans blowing snow from the blinding-white ridge. Webster set thrust to station-keeping. The turbines subsided to a low rumble, the anti-gravity rotor now inaudible.

Viper and *Cobra* peeled off and sank slowly, cautiously into the clouds, intent on aiding the nearby villages of the Khumbu, battered by the earthquake which had shaken the mighty mountain to its roots just forty-eight hours ago. Meanwhile, *Turbinia* lowered the 5th Gurkha platoon down to the summit on handlines. They had their own mission.

Moments later, they set foot on holy Sagarmāthā, where Earth's forehead touches heaven, and set about transporting the injured expedition down the mountain by more old-fashioned means.

The ship's Tesla Set crackled.

"Thank you, *Turbinia*! Dhanyabad, Flight-Captain Webster-ji, we could not have done this without you!"

Webster looked out the cockpit, peering down onto the mountain. The Jemadar and his men were looking up and waving, as were the oxygen-masked Sherpa mountaineers, the first men to reach the summit.

"Thapa-ji, my respects to you and your men. You are the real heroes. See you at base camp!"

Turbinia rose slowly, gently, vectored fans, and drifted cautiously down, down into the clouds, ready to join the relief effort far below.

A. Stuart Williams is an author and journalist from the region of England which inspired Tolkien's dark land of Mordor - the 'Black Country'.

Fascinated by science fiction, fantasy, weird pulp, and steampunk since the 1960s, he grew up in the Space Age, reading classic American pulps.

Previously published in magazines and newspapers, a computer journalist and local history author, Stuart studied photography before working in newspapers and local government, and now writes speculative fiction in multiple genres.

Currently working on several projects, Pro Se Productions in the USA aim to publish Stuart's collection 'Rings Around The Sun' in 2016.

Launch event photos
© LM Cooke.

Nepal photos ©
Steven C. Davis

Launch event photos
© LM Cooke.

Nepal photos ©
Steven C. Davis

Photo / Art / Imagery Credits

Craig Beas: pages 5, 30, 48, 49, 50, 53.

LM Cooke: page 49, 94, 95.

Kev Cooper: pages 62, 63.

Steven C. Davis: pages 10, 14, 18, 29, 43, 44, 50, 63, 68, 90, 94, 95.

S. J. Stewart: pages 72, 73, 74.

Miranda T.: pages 82, 83, 84, 85, 86.

Chelle Tovell: pages 23, 24.

'Raising Steam' guitar imagery pages 33, 34 – S. J. Stewart

Original launch event poster page 38 – LM Cooke

Southcart logo page 54 – The Image Designs

GASP logo page 57 – LM Cooke & Steven C. Davis

GASP logo page 58 – Steven C. Davis

Thanks & Dhanyabad

With thanks to Craig Beas, Thea Bradbury, Scott and Amy Carter, LM Cooke, Kev Cooper, Steven C. Davis, Theresa Derwin, Keith Errington, C. Carper-Leigh, Jon Hartless, James Josiah, I. I. Laverick, Lynne McCutcheon, Adrian Middleton, Adam Millard, Danielle Miller, S. J. Stewart, Miranda T., Chelle Tovell, Stu Tovell, A. Stuart Williams, C. S. Wright, and everyone who came to the launch day and everyone who's purchased a copy. Thank you.

Namaste